DISCIPLINING THE DUKE

BY

ANNABELLE WINTERS

COPYRIGHT NOTICE

Books by Annabelle Winters

The CURVES FOR SHEIKHS Series

Curves for the Sheikh
Flames for the Sheikh
Hostage for the Sheikh
Single for the Sheikh
Stockings for the Sheikh
Untouched for the Sheikh
Surrogate for the Sheikh
Stars for the Sheikh
Shelter for the Sheikh
Shared for the Sheikh
Assassin for the Sheikh
Privilege for the Sheikh
Ransomed for the Sheikh
Uncorked for the Sheikh
Haunted for the Sheikh
Grateful for the Sheikh
Mistletoe for the Sheikh
Fake for the Sheikh

The CURVES FOR SHIFTERS Series

Curves for the Dragon
Born for the Bear
Witch for the Wolf
Tamed for the Lion
Taken for the Tiger

The CURVY FOR HIM Series

The Teacher and the Trainer
The Librarian and the Cop
The Lawyer and the Cowboy
The Princess and the Pirate

The CEO and the Soldier
The Astronaut and the Alien
The Botanist and the Biker
The Psychic and the Senator

THE CURVY FOR THE HOLIDAYS SERIES
Taken on Thanksgiving
Captive for Christmas
Night Before New Year's
Vampire's Curvy Valentine
Flagged on the Fourth
Home for Halloween

THE CURVY FOR KEEPS SERIES
Summoned by the CEO
Given to the Groom
Traded to the Trucker
Punished by the Principal
Wifed by the Warlord

THE DRAGON'S CURVY MATE SERIES
Dragon's Curvy Assistant
Dragon's Curvy Banker
Dragon's Curvy Counselor
Dragon's Curvy Doctor
Dragon's Curvy Engineer
Dragon's Curvy Firefighter
Dragon's Curvy Gambler

THE CURVY IN COLLEGE SERIES
The Jock and the Genius
The Rockstar and the Recluse
The Dropout and the Debutante
The Player and the Princess
The Fratboy and the Feminist

WWW.ANNABELLEWINTERS.

DISCIPLINING THE DUKE

BY

ANNABELLE WINTERS

1

LONDON, ENGLAND
XYLA

"A Duke? Didn't you say he's American?"

The bald, clean-shaven lawyer straightens his gray tie which was exceedingly straight to begin with. It makes a metal clicking noise that strikes me as odd. "Indeed he *is* rather American," he says. "*Very* American. *Too* American. And that's where you come in. You've worked with Americans before, haven't you?"

I nod and pull at the hem of my long black business skirt. My hair feels stiff with hairspray and my bra is much too tight. Why is my bra tight? It wasn't tight a year ago when I bought it. I don't wear bras around the house and I don't wear hair-spray anywhere. Clearly I haven't left the house in a while. Clearly I'm nervous about this interview. Clearly I need this job.

The lawyer glances at the leather-bound folder that's got my qualifications neatly printed on thick white bond paper. It looks very proper. I'm very good at looking proper. I better be good at it: That's what I sell for a living. British "properness" and everything that goes into it.

"It says you've been a personal coach for over a decade," he says. His bald head comes up. His gray eyes are expressionless. Upper lip stiff like a day-old cucumber sandwich. He doesn't need coaching. "How old are you?"

"Old enough to handle an American brat who needs to be readied for Royalty," I say with a wry half-smile that I've practiced and taught. It goes well with British humor. And you can flash the smile when you take too big a bite from a cucumber sandwich and some green juice squirts onto your clean white blouse. That's only happened to me thrice. (Thrice means three times.) I don't wear white cotton to tea anymore. Green lambswool hides cucumber-swill best, I find. "How old is the young Duke, anyway? Eight? Ten? And an orphan?

No wonder he's acting up. No matter. Three months in my program and he'll be more royal than the Queen."

The lawyer frowns and raises a well-plucked left eyebrow. I shift my big bottom on the cool wood chair. "He doesn't *need* to be more royal than the Queen, Ms. Xyla. Dorshire is a non-royal Dukeship. My clients just need him to not be so . . . American." He blinks and I think he just glanced at my boobs. "Also, Mister Xavier is thirty-seven years old. He is indeed an orphan, but I wouldn't feel too sorry for him until you meet the man. Have you really not heard of him? I assumed you'd be all over the Social Media celebrity nonsense. Anyway, when you *do* meet him, Ms. Xyla, it's best if this arrangement is kept private. He's to think you're part of the dead Duke's manor staff. Part of the whole . . . thing."

My eyebrows move up and stay up. Thirty-seven years old? And what's with the fakery? I glance at my resume and wonder if he called my references. If he did, he'd know that I work with children and teens and the occasional animal when things get tight. I frown at the lawyer and take a closer look at his tie. It's a clip-on. Great. Just great. This has shadiness written all over it. Who are his clients?

Why did they pick me? Yes, my rates are cheap compared to a coach who actually works with *real* royalty that need tutelage on the ways of High Society, but is that the only reason I'm sitting in a clip-on-tie lawyer's offices?

Maybe I'm the only option, I think when I glance at a cream-colored sheet of paper on the lawyer's desk. It's got a long list of names on it and most of them are crossed out. Maybe every reputable coach turned down the offer. Maybe I'm the bottom of the barrel, the last resort, the only one dumb enough (or desperate enough—London rent isn't cheap, now that the Vikings aren't invading us anymore . . .) to ignore the shadiness of what's happening here.

Still, royalty has always had its shadiness and secrets. Royalty is all about perception, what others see of you and say of you and think of you. And he's right: Dorshire's Dukeship is pretty close to the bottom of the royal barrel. No family connection to Buckingham Palace. The clients are probably distant relatives who aren't in line for the Dukeship but still enjoy the connection and privilege. A privilege that they don't want revoked by a badly behaving American.

Still a bit shady, but really, what's the worst that can happen, I think as the lawyer clears his throat and then launches into a sales pitch like *he's* the one being interviewed. It only confirms my suspicions, but I'm savvy enough to know that if I start asking questions like the previous interviewees must have, my name could well be crossed out. Sure, if I really am the last option, I might try negotiating for more money. But you never know. Best I can see from here that list has a couple of names not crossed out. I'm in no financial position to look this gift horse in the mouth (even though it almost certainly has British teeth . . .). Besides, working with an honest-to-goodness Duke could open new doors for me if I pull it off.

In fact, if I play this right, this American Duke could be a jewel in the crown of my career.

A feather in my hat.

A notch in my belt.

2

<u>ONE WEEK LATER</u>
<u>MAYFAIR HOTEL</u>
<u>SOHO, LONDON</u>
<u>XAVIER</u>

Another notch in my belt, I think as my hotel-room door closes and I'm alone with my hangover. I sigh and glance at my brown belt on the rough carpet. There was a time when I actually *did* make little notches in the leather with a switchblade. Went all the way around that old belt before I ran out of space. Then I lost count. Lost control.

And finally lost myself.

I groan and rub my temples and bury my scruffy face in the pillow. The smell of that nameless, faceless blonde woman from the hotel bar sickens me, but not as much as that previous thought does: That I've lost myself. For years I've felt it festering in my chest like a sickness, and I feel it stronger now. I feel it in my aching head. I feel it in my empty heart. I feel it in my hollowed-out soul.

Or maybe it's just the hangover.

I lean off the side of the bed and retch. Nothing comes out. I'm dried out and hollow inside from years of drinking that's now way past the point of fun. It stops being fun when you don't remember what you did last night. Or who you did it with.

There's a knock on the door and I throw a pillow in its general direction. What's with the housekeeping at these London hotels? Why don't they pay attention to those fucking "Do Not Disturb" signs?

"Unless that hotel-bar harlot flipped the sign on the way out," I mutter, covering my ears and curling my long naked body into an overgrown fetus when the knock comes again. Three stern raps in quick succession and then one more with a flourish that makes me see red.

"Go away!" I shout. "It's seven in the fucking

morning! Don't you know I am your King? Off with their heads, Guards!"

"It's three in the afternoon, Mister Xavier," comes a woman's cheery British voice from beneath the doorframe and above the transom. There's a pregnant pause and I feel her swallow. Then she laughs with such British politeness that I almost smile. "We follow Greenwich Mean Time here, Mister Xavier. We're eight hours ahead of American Pacific Time."

Figured it out before I did, I think with grudging admiration. I glance at my wrist and frown when I don't see my Rolex. I look over at the bedside table but there's just a flute of flat Dom Perignon with a cherry-red lipstick stain on it. No fucking way. Blondie did *not* just steal my Rolex!

Now I leap out of bed and race to the door, pulling it open and dashing out into the hallway. I frantically look left and right as my head pounds. It's only when I feel the woman flinch and turn away from my nakedness that I realize I'm . . . well . . . naked.

"Fuck, sorry," I say, rubbing the back of my head and then scratching my beard. I glance down at my long cock and heavy balls. When I was younger I had a thing for getting naked when I was hammered. Didn't give a damn who saw what and how often. We're all animals, right? Born naked and all that. I glance towards the elevator lobby down the hall and frown. "You didn't by any chance see a . . ." I start to say before realizing that the hotel-bar burglar is long gone by now. Thank God I didn't actually fuck her. I didn't, did I? I glance down at myself. My cock is dry and clean and my balls feel full and heavy. Whatever happened last night didn't involve me blowing my load.

"I didn't see a thing," says the woman. "Not a thing. Nothing at all. Absolutely nothing. Might as well be blind. That's it! I'm blind. Didn't see a thing because I *can't* see a thing!"

Now I turn to this British babbler and look her up and down. She's got her eyes clamped shut so tight her face is scrunched up and puckered. She's very pretty, and her psycho-babble is almost cute. There's also something else about her, I realize as my gaze travels down along her strong hourglass shape and stops at her wide hips. My cock moves as I stare at how her black slacks hug those hips. It takes about two seconds for me to harden when the thought of my face in that British muff floods my mind. I've never been big on eating pussy, but damn I want to taste this Englishwoman's very proper cunt right now. Slide my filthy tongue all the way up in there, swirl it around and show her what American-style freedom is all about. She'd come on my face while saying something like *Egad* or *Milk-thistle* (I don't fucking know . . .). Then I'd flip her over and plant my Star Spangled Flagpole right in her tight English bum.

Now I'm grinning as my throbbing cock cures my hangover so well I feel kinda drunk right now. She's red in the face and her lips are moving. Hell, she's really freaked out by my nakedness, isn't she? I guess that's reasonable. Am I that jaded and de-sensitized that I don't consider public nakedness a problem?

Nah, that's not it, I think with a sigh as I turn and stroll back into my room. My pants are in a crumpled heap on the carpet. They feel light, and I groan when I see that my wallet's missing too. I'm less pissed about the wallet than the watch, though. I never carry any cards in my wallet. No ID or anything like that. I keep my passport and credit cards in a secure pouch that stays in my carry-on bag. My wallet's just for cash. I think I lost about nine hundred Pounds Sterling. That's quite a score for that bar-room bandit. Hell, maybe she'll retire from a life of sleaze. Though if she's sleazy, what does it make me?

It's a struggle to shove my swollen cock into my lambswool trousers but I manage to do it without

injury to man or beast. I don't see my shirt anywhere, but I think that's OK. I just saw Ms. Proper
peek and now she's got both eyes open.

"Hi," I say, reaching out my right hand and smiling broad. My teeth shine like diamonds and my
breath is always fresh. Alcohol does keep you clean
inside. "Who're you?"

"I sent you a message. I'm Xyla," she says, glancing at my hand and then blinking and demurring.
I frown and look down and then wince when I see
the smudge of that woman's lipstick circling my
middle finger like a ring. So she sucked my finger
last night? Man, these British chicks are weird.

My hangover pinches behind the eyes and I rub
my temples. "I get too many messages and so I don't
read any of them. Though your name sounds familiar. Xyla . . ." I say. "You're the . . . what are you
again?"

"The Help," she says cheerfully. "I'm the Chief
of Staff at your Dorshire Manor." She smiles and
shrugs. "Also the *only* staff right now. It's not a very
big estate. And your late uncle—may Duke Edward
rest in peace—didn't see the need for most of the
formalities."

"Clearly he saw the need for you," I say with a
raised eyebrow and a cocked head. I narrow my eyes

at her as something occurs to me. "Though I coulda sworn my uncle the dead Duke was gayer than the Queen's husband." I wink and flash a grin and lean in close. "The Queen's husband *is* gay, isn't he?" I whisper.

Xyla stares with the sort of horror that belongs on stage, and I realize she didn't get that I was messing with her. Fuck me. "Oh, right," I say with a sigh and a hand-swipe. "British humor is ironic. American sarcasm doesn't work here."

She blinks and swallows and then shakes her head. "That wasn't sarcasm. It was shock-humor. I don't think that works *anywhere*."

She smiles and winks and I grin and snap my fingers and point. "Excellent sarcasm," I acknowledge. "Now, is my carriage waiting downstairs? How many horses? I want ten horses. Maybe twelve."

"I hope you're being sarcastic," Xyla says. She eyes my bare chest disapprovingly and I put my hands on my hips and bite my lip. I'm not jacked like some meat-head with steroid-balls, but I'm lean and tight, with a well-defined six-pack and more real strength than most body-builders. "We'll be taking the train to Dorshire. Now, can we put some clothes on, please?"

"We?" I say with a chuckle as I try to push away an image of how big and red her nipples might be under all those layers of British propriety. "Oh, right. Now that I'm royalty, I get to use the royal *we*. Just like the Queen."

"You aren't royal like the Queen is royal," she says, following me into the room without being invited. Interesting. Maybe this woman isn't as shy and reticent as she makes out to be. What else is she hiding from me? Last time I saw Uncle Ed was before my folks died eleven years ago, but I seem to remember him being a loner to the extreme. Dad told me that it was because of the don't-ask, don't-tell nonsense of British High Society back in the day. Apparently it wasn't "proper" to be a gay Duke even though you gotta think that historically at least *some* of these men who dressed in furs and diamonds and pink stockings and white wigs marched to that other drumbeat.

Whatever, I think as I flip open my suitcase. The whole Royalty thing is a fucking joke anyway. In America we fought a bloody-ass war for the right to *not* have a Royal Class. I can't take this shit seriously.

And if I have my way, *nobody's* gonna take this shit seriously.

Not when they see me defile the Dukeship with my American arrogance and Yankee sensibilities. I'm not here for the fucking pomp and splendor,

I remind myself as I dig out my carefully curated attire and smile. I'm here to show the world that this shit is a joke, that Royalty belongs in the past along with all beliefs that make one class of people "better" than another.

There's a reason I spent years cultivating a Social Media presence that's founded on bad behavior and shock-you tactics, I think as I unfurl the cape of fake fur and sling it onto my bare shoulders. Then I pull out the diamond-studded choker that's so over-the-top I can barely keep a straight face with it on. I put it on and try to keep a straight face. Doesn't work, and I'm grinning like a Chelsea cat when I see Xyla's mouth hang open at my ensemble.

"I'm ready," I say firmly, sniffing my bare armpits and giving her a thumbs-up. I pull out my phone and click three quick selfies. I select the best one and shoot it out to all my Social Media channels. My phone starts to go nuts just as I turn off the notifications so it doesn't ping, beep, and throb all the way to Dorshire. "To my castle!" I proclaim. "Yee-haw! Here we go, baby! Down with the British Empire! America in the fucking *house*!"

3
XYLA

You *do* know that the UK is a democracy, not an *Empire*," I say as Xavier asks another mortified train-passenger how he feels about bending the knee to the British Crown like a pussy-whipped something-or-other. I smile apologetically as the last passenger in our section hastily gathers his brown coat and gray hat and exits at a stop that I suspect isn't his.

"Where'd everyone go?" Xavier says, slouching in the seat and raising his long legs that easily stretch across. He plants his feet on the seat-bench beside me. He's wearing Harley-Davidson branded boots that are scuffed in a way that make me think he actually does ride a motorbike. Also, his feet are very large. Come to think of it, the glimpse I got back at the hotel seemed to back up what they say about the correlation between a man's feet and his phallus.

He looks at me and grins again. He grins a lot, but the smiles are oddly genuine. Delightfully genuine. Xavier might be a thirty-seven year old man, but he acts like a child and seems to absolutely *love* it. It's infectious, but I'm not going to be infected. I barely acted like a child when I *was* a child. Besides, I'm being paid very handsomely (*surprisingly* so, which makes me even more confused and suspicious about Clip-on Lawyer . . .) to rein in the Duke's horses.

Moments after taking the job and getting the skinny on the new Duke, I'd found Xavier's Social Media channels and immediately understood why I'd been asked to pretend to be part of his dead uncle's staff or estate or whatever. He would never agree to a coach. Certainly never hire one himself. The man walked the talk—and both his walk and his talk were out there. Like *way* out there.

"Listen, Xavier," I say, pausing as two stiff-hatted train conductors stroll past us. They each raise at eyebrow at Xavier's bare-chested, fake-fur wearing, diamond-choker sporting attire. Then they grunt and walk on like they've seen better. Or worse.

"I'm a Duke, you know," Xavier calls after them.

One of them turns and grins. "And I'm the Queen's bloomers," he shoots back. The two conductors chuckle and pass through to the next car. Xavier twiddles his thumbs and sighs and shakes his head. "Royalty isn't what it used to be," he says.

I smile. "Thank heavens for that," I say without thinking.

Xavier pulls his feet off the seat and leans forward. "Why do you say that?"

I bite my lip and shrug. "I didn't mean to. I mean, I didn't mean anything by it."

He rubs his beard and grunts. Slowly he leans back and raises his feet again, keeping his green eyes trained on my face like he's watching for something. I blink and glance down at his boots.

"You ride a motorcycle?" I say quickly.

He glances at his boots and then back into my eyes. "Among other things."

I blink again as the color rises up my neck. I'd kept my eyes firmly shut outside the hotel room, but my body had felt the way he looked at me back there. I felt his gaze take in my curves, study my heavy bosom, rest on my wide hips. I didn't see his erection but I'd felt it. I don't know how I can know that but I do. I've never been a particularly sexual person, but back at the hotel I'd felt a wetness between my legs that I knew was arousal. I feel the wetness now too, like I've been oozing into my panties just from being around this cocky, brash American who seems to have his own agenda just like that lawyer and his mysterious clients.

Seems like everyone's got an agenda except me, I think as the train hisses to a stop at the next station. Nobody gets on. We're way out in the country now. Just two more stops to Dorshire. Then what happens? The manor is empty and the lawyer gave me the key, but the rest is up in the air. The lawyer was oddly non-prescriptive about that. Like all he cared about was me and Xavier getting to Dorshire.

"What happens when we get to Dorshire?" Xavier says after nobody he can terrorize enters our compartment. "Will there be a parade? Archery contests? Bullfighting?" He raises an eyebrow and twists his mouth. "Cockfighting?" he whispers.

I giggle even though I don't want to encourage him. "Is that something you enjoy?"

He grins. "Depends on the opponent."

I clear my throat and curl my hair around my ear. I shift my bottom on the smooth Rexine seat and wonder if there's a wet spot under me. Thankfully I'm wearing black. Another throat-clear and I lean over to my brown leather satchel and pull out the thick folder embossed with the Duke's Family Seal. Seeing that had given me some confidence that the lawyer was hired by someone connected to Dorshire. I'd assumed it was distant relatives, but I couldn't trace any in England. Duke Edward had a younger brother who moved to America when he was a teenager. Xavier is that brother's son.

"I'm sorry you lost your parents ten years ago," I say, flipping through the folder and stopping at a family photograph of a young Xavier with his father, mother, uncle, and another man. I frown and check the neatly printed caption. The man isn't listed. "Who's that?" I say, leaning forward so he can see. Xavier looks and then frowns.

He leans back and taps his lower lip. "My uncle's friend. Well, more than just a friend, I'd presume." He narrows his eyes and glances out the window. The meadows are turning brown. Winter is coming. "I'd forgotten about him," he says softly, still staring out the window. He's quiet for a while and then he looks at me and smiles. It's not that diamond-bright, who-gives-a-damn smile. There's a sadness in the smile, and I'm startled when I glimpse an emotional depth that I'd thought didn't exist but was perhaps just well hidden. He doesn't say more about the man and I don't ask. If he was the late Duke's partner, then perhaps I'd be expected to know him, wouldn't I? But something tells me that's not the whole story. And why would Xavier have "forgotten" about him? Is that mystery-man the lawyer's mysterious client? Shit, maybe he's the lawyer himself!

I take a closer look at the photograph. The man in the picture has thick dark hair and a manicured goatee. I try to imagine him bald and clean shaven. With a clip-on tie. Nope. No way the elegant man in the picture wears a clip-on tie.

Now I slam the folio closed and grit my teeth as I meet Xavier's gaze and then look away. Suddenly I want to open up to him, tell him that I never knew his uncle, that I've been hired by some shady lawyer, that I'm being paid to "coach" the new Duke. The lawyer wasn't clear on what that meant. He'd handed me this thick folder with the official seal and told me I'd find everything I needed in there. He was wrong. I didn't find everything I needed in there. There was almost nothing in there. The "dossier" was the research equivalent of a clip-on tie.

"One more stop and then us," I say. Xavier nods

and pulls out his phone. I've been following his feeds for the past week, and I know what he's doing. I know what he is.

"You ever considered becoming a Social Media Celebrity?" he says, turning the phone towards me as my heart speeds up and I hurriedly cover my face. "I can show you how to make money doing it. A lot of fucking money."

"Don't. Please," I say, spreading my fingers to peek and then closing up again. I don't do cameras. My Social Media profiles all have one of those computer-generated cartoons that sort of look like you (but thinner).

"Relax," he says, putting away the phone and softening his gaze when he sees how anxious I just got. "I didn't click. Wouldn't do it without permission. Besides, my feeds only have pictures of me. That's my thing."

"I noticed," I say, uncovering my face as the train slows. I look up at our bags in the metal overhead rack. Mine is a cheap black roller with a faded yellow safety-check sticker from when I took it to Spain on a college trip. Xavier carries a Louis Vuitton suitcase that makes me wonder how much money a Social Media Celebrity can make.

I frown and tap my lip as I wonder how much

more money Xavier will make now that he's a Duke. Well, he isn't a Duke yet, technically. Not until the ceremony in two weeks. A ceremony that will hopefully happen without any waves, with all the seriousness and splendor that befits the position. Because if Duke Xavier proves that he's willing to take this seriously, to not make this a series of inane images on Instagram or a rant against royalty on Reddit, then maybe . . . just *maybe* . . . he gets invited to a reception at Buckingham Palace.

A meeting with the Queen.

Shivers rise up my back as I think back to when my mum and dad took me to Buckingham Palace. I'd stared in fascination at the statuesque Beefeaters, watched in wonder as we walked through the gilded halls of history. I'd loved everything about it back then. Of course, when I grew up I understood that royalty was a thing of the past, that I very much want a world where class and race and sexual orientation aren't dividing lines between people. But there's still something about the ritual of royalty that gets to me. Something about the seriousness of the ceremony, how we all play along like it's make-believe, a bunch of grown-ups pretending like we're dolls in a doll-house. Is that so bad sometimes? Am I old-fashioned and pathetic for believing that? For feeling that?

"Feel that?" Xavier says as the train squeaks to a stop. He cups his hand to his ear and looks up. "That's what fate feels like, Xyla. That's what destiny feels like."

I snort quizzically. "What are you talking about? Come on. The train won't stop here long."

Xavier rises and pulls both bags off the rack. I try to take my ugly black roller from him but he grunts and shakes his head. His six-pack abs flex as he lifts my heavy suitcase over the seat and effortlessly strides to the door. I hurry after him with my satchel. The platform is low, and I stop at the door to sling my satchel across my shoulders so I can hold the siderails and step down in my modest heels that I don't wear much.

Just then the train releases its brakes with a hiss, and I panic as an old fear tightens my throat and makes me dizzy. My fingers close tight around the siderails and my heart beats wildly as the train slowly starts to move.

"Hey! Hop off! What are you doing?" comes Xavier's voice. Now he's shouting towards the front of the train but the engine is too far ahead. In three long strides he's alongside the open door, holding out his arm as he keeps pace with surprising ease. His long legs move effortlessly like an antelope on the run, and the way his fake-fur cape flows behind him makes him look like a super-hero in a goofy arthouse film. "Come on. I got you, Xyla."

I look at him and then down at the platform. It's moving awfully fast. "I'll get off at the next stop and take the train going the other direction," I say, trying to stay calm even as that memory of being mistakenly left behind by mum and dad makes my voice tremble, makes my knees buckle. I swallow hard and prepare to step back from the door, but before I can do it Xavier steps up the pace and reaches for my waist and yanks me out and into his arms with an easy strength that's so unexpected I gasp.

The train's whistle sounds as I loop my arms around his neck. My fingers touch the diamond choker that's so obscenely obtrusive it makes me want to laugh.

I actually *do* laugh—partly from the sudden release of anxiety and partly because I feel strangely giddy, happy like I haven't in years. Xavier stops at the end of the platform, me in his arms, both our heads turned to watch the train disappear down the tracks like a long silver snake. Then we turn back to each other and now we're looking into one another's eyes and I feel that giddiness again, that happiness again, a weird flutter behind my breast that feels like . . . it feels like . . . like . . .

I blink as the thought puzzles me, and I'm about to say something but I can't.

I can't because something just happened.

Something that makes no sense.

Something that feels like we're playing make believe, like we're just dolls in a dollhouse, actors on a stage.

He kisses me.

Out of nowhere, he kisses me.

Firm on the lips.

Hard on the mouth.

Smack on the face.

He kisses me.

By God, he kisses me.

4
__XAVIER__

I didn't mean to kiss her but I did kiss her and now it's done. Like posting something online, you can't truly undo it. It lives forever even if you pretend like it never happened. So why pretend? I kissed her. So what? She isn't married, is she?

"You aren't married, are you?" I say as the black taxicab slowly circles the frontice-round after dropping us at the entrance to the Duke of Dorshire's Manor. It's smaller than the images I found online, but in a way feels grander. It had looked a murky brown in the photos, but as the evening sun hits the vine-covered west wall, the manor shines gold and green like this is a dream.

"No. I am not married," says Xyla. She touches her mouth and glares down at her black rollerbag on the stone entryway. She doesn't look at me. She doesn't say anything else. She just snaps up the handle and rolls her bag to the door. It's locked.

I stand back and slide my hands into my pockets as she fumbles in her satchel. She pulls out a brown envelope and opens it. A large brass key slips out. It falls on the floor and she picks it up, taking care to bend her knees so I don't get to look at her ass. She's tense as hell. And you know what?

So am I.

"Listen, Xyla . . ." I start to say, exhaling slow and frowning as she sticks the big brass key into the even bigger oak door and turns. Nothing happens and my frown cuts deeper. Doesn't she live here? She was on my uncle's staff, wasn't she? Why was the key in a brown envelope? Why does she not know how to unlock the door? Why is she so tense? Why am *I* so fucking tense?

Now Xyla drops the key again, and when she turns I see her eyes and I drop my bag and stride to the door. I bend for the key and she bends too and our heads bump and we stand up together and rub our foreheads and look at each other. The key looks up at us from the ground.

"I'll get it," I say. She nods and I pick up the key. It's heavy and old, and it feels warm in my palm. I close my fingers over it and think about what I'd said when the train stopped. *This is what fate feels like*, I'd said to her or maybe to myself. Perhaps to both of us. *This is what destiny feels like.*

The key fits perfectly and makes a satisfying click when I turn it. The door swings open silently, and the aroma of the manor greets us. I step inside and take a deep breath. It smells like my uncle, I think. English leather and lavender soap. That's what he always smelled like.

"You coming?" I say when I notice Xyla's shadow motionless in the doorway. I turn and hold my arm out. "Come on. Show me your room."

Xyla stares and I see the panic in her big brown eyes. This is more than just awkwardness from the kiss. I put my hands on my hips and meet her gaze.

"You don't live here, do you?" I say quietly. "You never did."

She blinks about forty times and swallows so hard I wonder if she'll choke. She doesn't choke, but she doesn't speak either. She just nods once and looks down at the floor like a guilty schoolgirl.

"And you never worked for my uncle," I say, taking another step towards her. "You've never even been to Dorshire." Two more steps and I'm close enough to smell her. No perfume but a strong essence of sweet orange. She even tasted like an orange—sweet but with a edge. I want to kiss her again. Why can't I kiss her again? I'm going to kiss her again.

I reach out and touch her hair and she slaps my hand away and steps back. I grin and take her hand in mine, but she pulls away and crosses her arms over her boobs and juts her lower lip out like she's about to cry. I sigh and hold my arms out to the sides.

"You going to talk or do I have to guess?" I say.

She shakes her head and looks down at the floor. "Your guess is as good as mine," she says. She peers up at me now, and I see the hint of a smile on her dark red lips. "Maybe even better than mine. Are *you* behind this? Did you secretly hire that lawyer to secretly hire me?"

"Sure," I say, glancing up at a chandelier the size of a Volkswagen. The bulbs are old-world incandescent, and I wonder if they still work. There's a gold-threaded cord hanging down from it and I pull on it. Every bulb lights up and suddenly it's like we're under golden starlight. I pull out my phone and step back to capture a selfie taken from below. Witty caption. Upload. Done.

"It *was* you, wasn't it?" she says, glancing at my phone and then up at my face. "This is some weird publicity stunt. You planned all of this. You've been planning it for years." She reaches into her satchel and pulls out that leather folio with that old picture of me and my folks and Uncle Ed and his quiet, elegant friend whose name escapes me. "Your father and Duke Edward were brothers. Your father stayed a British Citizen even after moving to America, so he would have been in line for the Dukeship if he'd been alive." She pulls open the folder and flips through the pages like she knows what she's looking for. She holds up a page. It's a copy of my British Passport. "You were born a dual citizen of the UK and the US," she says. "So when your father died, you must have figured that you were now the heir to the Dukeship of Dorshire. You'd have known that eleven years ago."

She thumbs through my dossier like a studious detective in a bad BBC show that's way too slow for American audiences. This is when you need someone storming onto the scene with a gun. That, or I need to kiss her again. Just fucking kiss her, you idiot. Kings banged the help all the time, didn't they? Chambermaids, scullerymaids, minutemaids. What's a minutemaid? Fuck if I know. Just kiss her.

I'm about to do just that when she holds up the hard-backed folder and almost hits me in the face with it. I stop just in time and blink at the open page. It's too close to my face for me to read.

"So what if I knew eleven years ago?" I say, stepping back and squinting at the page. "Is that . . . is that my first Social Media post?"

"Ten years ago," she says. "You were twenty-six. A star lawyer at a white-shoe Manhattan law firm. Then your parents died in a car crash and a year later you quit your job and went off the deep end . . . in public."

I grin and run my hand through my hair. "*Dived* off the deep end is more like it," I say with a flip of the head and my trademark raised left eyebrow. "I found my calling and chased it. Had my midlife crisis a bit early. What's your point? You going somewhere with this, Ms. Investigator?" I grin and look up at the chandelier and then down at her. "Ohmygod, did I kill my father to clear the path to the throne of . . . Dorshire?" I say in a comically menacing growl. Then I rub my chin and put my pinky in my mouth. "But then why would I wait ten years for Uncle Ed to die of natural causes? It would have been *so* much simpler to arrange for him to die in a . . . I dunno . . . fox-hunt accident or something."

"I . . . I . . ." she says, biting her lip and frowning at the dossier of yours truly prepared by Her Majesty's Secret Serpent. Serpent? Doesn't sound right but whatever. She closes the folder and holds it against her chest. Then she sighs and looks up at me. "This is mad. Bonkers. I should have my head checked for agreeing to this. I should just beg out before I'm in too deep. To hell with the money. I'll just go back to working with animals. There's nothing wrong with that, is there?"

She looks at me and I shrug. "Is that a real question?" I say.

"No," she says. "None of this feels real. That lawyer had a clip-on tie. Who wears clip-on ties?"

I rub my diamond choker and frown. Then I hold my hand out and look at my fingers. "Maybe he didn't have fingers. Did you see his fingers?"

Xyla thinks a moment. "Actually he wore gloves—which I suppose is sort of strange," she says. Then she flashes a smile that's vaguely admiring. "But that's a good guess, actually. Who wears a clip-on tie? Why, a man who can't tie a knot, of course! A man without fingers!"

I chuckle and step past Xyla towards the open door. I lean out, look left and right, and then close the door and slide the black iron deadbolt. "So now we have a man without fingers who hired you on behalf of a secret client to pretend to be part of Uncle Ed's staff to get close to me." I turn and smile. "Which you've managed to do—and quite well. So is now when you kill me?"

Xyla touches her lower lip and blinks. She tugs on the satchel strap that's slid between her breasts. She looks hot as fuck. I hope she isn't an assassin. But speaking of ass, she's got a killer rear end. Big and round and bouncy. I want to bounce her on my cock.

"But why?" she says.

I'm about to answer that it would be fun to have her bounce on my cock, that's why. Sadly that wasn't the question. I glance at my watch and then remember it was stolen this morning along with my wallet. Was that a coincidence? Is any of this a coincidence? Is any of this even real?

We're both quiet as the questions hang above us like the spiderweb arms of that chandelier. I think back over the day and it occurs to me that every-thing could have been engineered and scripted except for one thing.

There's one thing that couldn't have been planned. I know it because I felt it.

And it felt like fate.

It felt like destiny.

It felt real.

Perhaps the only thing that's real.

5
XYLA

That kiss felt real, and it's messing me up. I don't know if Xavier's masterminding this whole thing, but I do know that kiss wasn't part of the plan.

I touch my lip again as I watch Xavier stride across the Great Hall of the Dorshire Manor. The fake fur cape catches the yellow light from the chandelier and casts Xavier in a golden glow which doesn't help make this thing feel any more real. My mind spins as Xavier holds his arms out and laughs up at the high ceiling with the carefree delight of a madman. I can see he's been thinking about this for years, slowly and methodically building a Social Media platform that he could use when the time came. What does he plan to do with it, though? There have already been articles about him becoming a Duke, but since Dorshire is a sleepy old country town where even the locals aren't particularly interested in the whole affair, the news got swept away when the next wave of Kanye and the Kardashians hit the news cycle. Big publications like the *New York Times* or the *London Times* barely gave the story a footnote, and although Xavier's been posting images all day, the captions have been teasers with nothing made clear. I'd bet most of his followers haven't quite realized what's happening. Not yet, at least. Xavier's building up to something, isn't he? The big reveal. The grand finale. The magical moment of shock and awe. Am I part of that moment? Do I *want* to be part of that moment? Do I have a choice?

"Uncle Ed made some interesting choices with the decor," Xavier says from the far end of the hall. "Come here. Look at this."

I glance up at the grand staircase of smooth polished oak that winds up to the bedrooms. I push away the memory of that kiss and follow his voice. When I see him Xavier's got his back to me and he's staring at a painting so big it covers most of the wall. I could do a starfish impersonation on the canvas and my fingers wouldn't touch the frame. I think of Clip-on Lawyer's fingers beneath those gloves. Did he have stubs for hands? Gnarled claws like the Loch Ness Monster?

"A fucking monstrosity," Xavier mutters, his eyebrows raised at the gaudy painting that's a cross between Dante's *Inferno* and Enid Blyton's *Noddy*. Mythical creatures with grotesque blue beaks and black tentacles play croquet with toy soldiers with painted-on smiles. "If this was his life's work, no wonder Uncle Ed killed himself."

I jerk my head towards Xavier, a chill running down my backbone. "That's not right. The Duke died of natural causes."

Xavier doesn't flinch. "Yes, I know," he says, his gaze fixed on the painting. He stares and then blinks and looks at me. "But my version makes for a better joke." He grins and winks at my shock. "What? In today's world you can invent the truth so it fits the story," he says. "Nobody has time to fact-check. Even if they do, nobody gives a shit. We believe anything posted by a famous person. Doesn't matter if we don't even remember why that person is famous."

"Talking about yourself, I presume?" I say as I shudder at the painting and then turn away and

glance towards the open end of the Great Hall.
There are four old oakwood chairs with high backs
and leather seats worn smooth. An alcove with
three purple paisley divans arranged in a crescent
around an ivory-topped table. Colorful but not gaudy. The painting feels out of place. Or maybe it's me
that's out of place. Why am I still here?

Because I've already been paid in full and I've
already spent half the money to catch up on rent
and credit card bills. Now I understand why people
in movies do such stupid things for a little bit of
money. Money has power over you even after you
spend it. Maybe more so after you spend it.

Maybe I can do one night and then return half the
money, I think. Xavier walks past me and I glance
at his diamond choker and wonder if it's real. Again
that sense of un-realness washes over me and I hurry after him before the monsters from that painting
come alive and pull me into their world.

"I'm famous because I give people something to
look at," Xavier says as we walk to the paisley divans. He takes the middle one and drapes his long,
lean body over it with relaxed grace. I look at his
flat stomach and into his green eyes and at his red
lips. He catches me looking at him and smiles and I
quickly look down and touch my hair. I don't know

what to do now. That kiss destroyed my reality. It was so out of the blue that I want to believe it was orchestrated, part of his plan, captured on camera for some future purpose that only makes sense in the world of Social Media and attention-seeking madness.

Except it felt real. It felt more than real. *Sur*real. Extra-real. Maddeningly real.

"Did my mad old Uncle have a wine cellar, you think?" he says suddenly, his eyes lighting up as he looks past me. I turn and see a narrow staircase leading to the bowels of the manor. When I look back at the divan it's empty. Xavier's already at the stairs and he's gone in a flurry of fake fur.

I dig my satchel strap out from between my boobs and follow him to the cellar. It's dark and the air is stale but there's no dust. I cautiously wind my way down and then sigh when I see Xavier grinning like an idiot, posing like a fool against a row of old oak-wood vats that date back a hundred years. He snaps a photograph and teases his short-attention-span audience with what I admit is quite a pretty sight. I don't drink much, but when I do, it's red wine, the older the better.

"Gosh, this is old wine," I say, gasping when I see a vat dated 1879. I knock on the wood and listen. "Sounds full," I say, my eyes going wide when I count at least a dozen vats lined up in the cool, dark cellar. "These are worth a lot. If the wine is still good, of course."

"Let's check, shall we?" Xavier says. He looks around and then points. I turn and see a shelf with two clean glasses, long-stemmed and turned upside down on leather coasters. "Come on. Earn your keep, Chambermaid."

I raise an eyebrow and then sigh and pluck the glasses off the shelf. Alcohol is probably the *worst* idea right now, I think as Xavier takes the glasses and strolls down the line of vats. He stops halfway down and turns his head and grins. "Look at that," he says. "1776. Now *that* was a good fucking year." He flips the tap lever and the wine pours dark and syrupy. He pours a splash and swirls it and sniffs it and tastes it and grunts. Then he fills both glasses to the three-quarter mark and saunters back to me, the diamond choker catching the dim light from the incandescent bulbs lining the low wood ceiling.

"Why was 1776 a good year?" I say, taking the glass even as I remind myself that getting tipsy with so many unanswered questions is pretty dumb. Then I think that maybe a little wine might answer some questions in the way that sometimes when you're drunk things make *so* much sense. Of course, when you sober up you see it was all non-sense, but that happens later. Maybe never, if I'm lucky.

"You don't know your American history," Xavier says, coming close and putting his wine-glass arm through mine. "Though Americans winning their freedom from the Crown in 1776 is also British history, of course. But nobody wants to remember the bad shit that happened to them. Cheers. Drink up."

He curls his arm and brings the glass to his lips, pulling me closer in the bargain. I do the same, and we take our first sips together. I purse my lips and tighten my throat, not sure what to expect. I needn't have worried. The wine is still good.

We're still good too, I realize as we drain the glasses and flash wine-blackened smiles at each other. The buzz moves in fast but pleasantly, and I'm still smiling when Xavier hands me my refilled glass and raises his own. He swallows and I sip, and soon I'm two or three glasses behind him but buzzing like a beehive.

"I should stop," I say, my cheeks flushing from the wine, my eyes sparkling from my smile. I hiccup and cover my mouth and giggle and hiccup again. I hold my half-finished glass out and shake my head.

Xavier laughs and takes the glass from me so I can attend to my giggle-cups.

"I know a surefire cure for the hiccups," he says, finishing his glass and then draining the dregs of my glass. He turns both glasses over and holds them by the stems. They clink sweetly and I giggle again and hiccup three more times.

I turn away from him, my cheeks burning from red wine and redder embarrassment. My shoulders shake as I hiccup again, and now I'm getting flustered and I'm feeling drunk and my damned bra is *so* tight and there are *so* many questions and that kiss was *so* nice and his lips were *so* warm and ohmygod I'm going to die in this cellar and ohmygoodness I'm going to be eaten by those monsters and ohmylord I'm going to . . . I'm going to . . . I'm going to . . .

Now I feel him behind me and he turns me and I look at him. He's got diamonds around his throat and stars in his eyes. His fur catches the light and his smile catches my breath. My bra feels tighter than ever and I would like to take it off, thank you very much. I look up at him and gulp down the thick aftertaste of sweet old wine. A hiccup comes and goes and I barely notice. Xavier touches my cheek with the back of his hand and I most definitely notice. His fingers are long and his hand is big and his skin is rough like he's worked with his hands before, knows how to use those fingers. He draws close enough that I feel his breath warm and wonderful against my lips. I'm looking up at him and I shudder when I feel his long left arm slide around my wide waist. He pulls me close and we look at each other.

"When I kissed you at the train . . ." he whispers, his voice thick with wine and something else. I feel him hard and big against me, and I try to remember why this is a terrible idea, why it was a terrible idea to take that glass, to take a sip, to take the chance.

He doesn't finish the sentence and I don't know if I want him to finish the sentence. The cellar is bathed in soft light and feels cozy and brown with the dark oakwood and low ceiling and no windows and no clocks. We could be anywhere in time, everywhere in space. Perhaps that wine took us back to 1776 or 1897 or last week or yesterday. Perhaps that kiss catapulted us to a future world or a parallel universe or an imaginary adventure. Maybe the wine really was bad and we're dead and in that painting now, spinning starfish-like through surreal swirls of gaudy color. I smile and swoon and I remember how it felt to be a girl outside Buckingham Palace and lost in the magic of make-believe, reveling in the radiance of Royalty. I understand now like I understood then that everyone is part of that ceremony, that splendor, that magic. Sometimes the orphans in the filthy rags take more delight in the procession than the bored princes and princesses who are trapped by their titles, slaves to their scepters, bound by their birthright.

My thoughts spin and my head spins and my feet spin and he's kissing me now. He's kissing me and I'm kissing him back. We're the Duke and the Duchess, I decide as our tongues touch and his arm pulls me closer and my bra feels tighter and I can barely breathe and my hiccups are gone. He isn't Xavier and I'm not Xyla and this isn't a dream because, like he said, you can invent the truth to fit the story in your head, can't you?

"I think you can," I whisper as he breaks from the kiss so we can breathe and look at each other and breathe again. He nods like what I said makes sense and he smiles and I smile and he strokes my cheek and kisses me gently. Then he kisses me harder and his hand slides down past my waist and he firmly grasps my bottom. He's so big and hard against me I can't believe it, and I think back to when he stormed out naked in the hotel hallway, his cock swinging like Big Ben striking twelve, his balls heavy like the Tower's bells.

Now I'm thinking of clocks and time, and when Xavier pulls back and touches my face I see a tan-line on his wrist where a watch should be. There's no watch and I frown as my head spins and suddenly I remember crossing paths with a tarted up blonde in the hotel clutching a Rolex bigger than her head.

"Where's your watch?" I slur through my sticky lips. His hand is on my bottom and his taste is in my mouth and now I feel like that tart, smell like that slut, wonder if I'm nothing more than a chambermaid or a scullerymaid or a minutemaid—whatever that is.

I try to push him away but he kisses me again. I'm thinking about that telltale tan-line and the missing watch, and it's all mixing with the colors of that painting, and now I imagine a fingerless lawyer with a clip-on tie smiling at me, and my hiccups are back, and I push Xavier away again and hiccup again and finally turn just in time so I don't throw up all over the Duke's fake fur.

6
XAVIER

"It's fake fur. Don't worry. Let it all out, Xyla. Come on. It's all right. I got you." My words slur and my head spins but she's clearly worse off. Gently I hold her long dark hair up and back so she doesn't puke all over it. She got some on my cape but that's all right. Now that I'm royalty, I can't be seen in the same cape twice, can I?

Xyla yaks again and hurls like she means it, her body heaving, her neck jerking. It doesn't bother me. I've been there so many times I could be giving lectures on how to puke with style and class. I stroke her hair as she dry-retches one last time and then gasps wildly. I help her straighten up.

She sways and grabs my diamond choker to stay upright. I pull her into me, still stroking her hair. The contact feels nice. I could do this forever. Hold her forever. Touch her hair and comfort her forever.

Her breathing slows and I pull my hand back to wipe the tears from her smooth cheeks. She glances down at the tan-line on my wrist and I remember her question about the watch. I bite my lip and wish I could go back a day, go back a night, ignore that blonde with enough face-paint to step into a Broadway chorus line. It shouldn't matter but it does. It matters because Xyla matters. Why does Xyla matter? I've only known her one damned day.

"Let's go upstairs," I say softly. "Get you some water. Maybe some air. Come. Can you walk?"

"Can *you* walk?" she gurgles when I take a step and almost trip over the stairs. She grabs my diamond-studded collar and pulls. I gag and laugh at the same time, rolling my eyes up and sticking my tongue out. She shrieks and I guffaw, and then I bend down and lift her into my arms and run up the stairs so fast she shrieks again.

We're both panting when I get her upstairs, but we're also both smiling. She looks so pretty I want to kiss her again. Maybe it's the wine, but I know what that feels like and it sure as hell doesn't feel like this. Whatever I felt when I kissed her on the platform is still in me and is only getting stronger.

I carry her through the Great Hall and past that gigantic painting which looks better now that I'm drunk. She's got her arms looped around my neck and I grin and hope to hell she doesn't ask me about the watch again. I should just tell her about that, I think. Why wouldn't I tell her about that? It was nothing. Even if I'd fucked that blonde it would mean nothing. I was single last night and so I . . .

My thoughts trail off when I realize that I'm still single, aren't I? Of course I am.

So why does it feel like I'm already with Xyla?

Why does it feel like she's already mine?

I carry her through the dining room that's got a solemn wooden table running lengthwise down the middle like a landing strip. We walk through the kitchen and past the man leaning against the wall and puffing on a pipe. I get to the back door leading to the grounds and then stop and turn.

"Who the fuck are you?" I say when it occurs to me that yeah, I just passed a man in the kitchen smoking a pipe. I feel sober suddenly, and Xyla's hiccuping softly but standing straight and steady. She looks at me and then at him and then at me again. I take a step forward and stop in front of Xyla. She relaxes somewhat, and I focus on the man. "I said, who the *fuck* are you?!"

The man smiles thinly and his smooth face crinkles in a way that tells me he's older than I thought. Full head of hair and dressed in a three-piece fitted suit, brown with a brass-buttoned waistcoat that's closed all the way up his wiry frame. His eyes are light gray and very much alive. They're also familiar.

"I'm the man with the gun," he says, pulling the pipe from his lips and exhaling sweet-smelling smoke that isn't harsh like tobacco. "Nice to see you again, Xavier. You don't recognize me, do you? No matter. We only met once."

"The photograph," says Xyla, closing one eye and examining him with the other. "You were with the old Duke. I mean, you were his . . . um . . ."

"Yes and yes," says the man, smiling at Xyla and then looking at me. I glance down and see a bulge beneath his jacket, right where a shoulder-holster might be. I think back to my inside-voice quip about how any moment I expected a man with a gun to walk onto the scene. Did I say that out loud? Did thinking it make it happen?

"Do you live here?" says Xyla. She extends her right hand and the man shakes it politely and gives her a courteous bow. "Did you hire the lawyer?"

"No and no," says the man, his gray eyes smiling though his lips don't move. "But I used to live here with Edward. And I know who hired the lawyer." He smiles and winks and leans close to Xyla. "He isn't really a lawyer, you know. Did you notice the clip-on tie?"

"Indeed," says Xyla, beaming at him and smiling like she's proud. She looks at me and then back at the man. "Is it because he doesn't have fingers?" she whispers excitedly.

The man almost chokes on his pipe. "Why on earth would you think that? He has *plenty* of fingers, I assure you. Stop being silly. There's no need to complicate something so simple with unnecessary silliness. No fingers! Absurd! How would he assassinate anyone without fingers? By sticking his stump-arms up their arse? This isn't a Monty Python sketch, you know."

Xyla covers her mouth and giggles hard and then hiccups softly. I match the man's raised eyebrow with my own. "Americans don't watch Monty Python," I snarl. "Now explain what you're doing here or I'll *make* you explain." I don't know why I said that to a man with a shoulder-holster but it seemed appropriately silly. After all, I'm an American Duke in a fake-fur cape and drunk off my ass on old English wine. This man is just par for the course my life seems to have taken. Shit, I should get a photo of this for my fans! Though maybe I should hold off and see what he says. Maybe he's camera shy but not gun shy. He might not react well to my iPhone flash.

The man takes a leisurely puff on his pipe and Xyla hiccups again. He glances disdainfully at my diamonds and fake fur cape and bare chest. He isn't scared of me. I wouldn't be scared of me either. Nobody's scaring anybody in this scene.

"That's a bit scary," Xyla says slowly. She looks at me and then back at the man. "Are you joking or is the clip-on lawyer really an assassin?"

I scratch an itch above my eye. My head hurts. I could use some coffee. Or more wine.

"We're all assassins in this business," the man says drolly. He looks at his pipe, frowns, and then empties the bowl into the blackstone sink. He blows out the ashes and taps it clean and slides it into his waistcoat pocket. Then he sighs and holds his hand out for me to shake. I do it without breaking eye contact. Silliness aside, this man is for real. I remember meeting him all those years ago, but I don't remember him saying a damned thing. I always figured he was Uncle Ed's lover, but looking back to that one meeting, he acted as much bodyguard as boyfriend.

"What business is that?" Xyla says, biting her lip and then gasping and snapping her fingers. "Oh, that's right! The *assassination* business!"

I groan and rub my temples. She's still drunk. So am I, for that matter. This isn't going to end well.

The man sighs and shakes his head. "You've heard of MI-6, I presume?"

Xyla gasps again. "Her Majesty's Secret Service?"

"You're fucking kidding me, right?" I snort.

The man looks blankly at us and then nods. "Why is that so unbelievable? MI-5 and MI-6 agents get assigned to all royal and not-so-royal houses. I've been assigned to the House of Dorshire. I served Edward. I would have served your father if he'd lived to become Duke. Now you're to become the Duke of Dorshire, Xavier, so now I serve you. You don't have any executive political power, but you're still a public figure. Protecting you is important."

"Yeah, I don't think I need protection," I say with a chuckle and a head-shake, crossing my arms over my bare chest and sighing.

The man smiles, and for a moment he looks his age. "You do. You have for a long time. And you will for the rest of your life. Which hopefully will be longer than some people want."

I rub my beard as my wine-soaked brain deciphers his words. I cock my head and stare. "Wait, you've *already* had to protect me? When? From whom?"

The man chuckles but not because anything's funny. "Why weren't you in that car with your parents eleven years ago when they got run off the road?" he says softly.

My frown cuts so deep it hurts. "Run off the road?" I say slowly as dread rises from my chest and grips my throat. "You mean someone ran them off the road? They said Dad was drunk and blew through the railing." The man doesn't respond and I blink and return to his question. "I'd broken my leg the night before the trip. I was supposed to go with them." I bite my lip and shake my head. "I got hammered on rye whiskey the night before and woke up in the hospital with a cast on my leg."

The man leans toward me. His whisper comes crisp and measured. "Clean break, wasn't it? Healed perfectly, didn't it?" Then he winks grimly. "You're welcome," he adds.

I blink so many times it feels like my eyelids might fly away. "That's ridiculous," I say, looking at Xyla almost like I'm pleading for her to agree with me. She isn't slap-happy anymore, and from the way she's looking at the man I can tell she believes him.

For a moment I wonder if Xyla is part of this thing as well. And now suddenly I feel alone and cornered, and I instinctively back away and wonder what the hell is going on here. Why would anyone kill my parents and me? Why would British Secret Service save my American ass? And from whom?

"It *is* a bit ridiculous," says the man matter-of-factly. "Especially since I was protecting you from . . . well . . . me."

Xyla and I both gawk like our eyeballs are on a synchronized swim team. The man seems pleased with himself. Maybe this *is* a Monty Python sketch. Or a British-style assassination where the villain takes his time explaining everything before pulling the trigger. Very considerate, these Brits.

"Don't worry," says the man. "They still think I'm working for MI-6. Which I am, of course—but not exclusively."

Xyla gets it before I do. "So you're a . . . a mole? A rat?"

The man scowls at her. "No need to be insulting. Double agent is the polite term." He straightens his tailored jacket and adjusts his waistcoat. "And although I'm not doing it for the money, the CIA *does* pay handsomely. This suit was tailored in Paris, you know. The French aren't good for much, but they do know how to cut a damn fine suit."

I try to massage my neck but feel that damned choker. I try to undo the clasp but can't get it right and give up on it. I don't think it matters. The choking feeling isn't from the choker. It's from inside me.

"Aren't the CIA and MI-6 on the same side?" I ask.

"Only when it comes to ISIS, Russia, and the French," says the man. "Otherwise it's every nation for itself. Hedge your bets and all that."

"So MI-6 assassinated his parents?" Xyla asks.

"Yes. There's an old-line faction in MI-6 that hates the idea of an American occupying even a low-level position in British Aristocracy. They wanted to get all three of you, though," he says, glancing at my left leg. "Wipe out your line. They would've tried again, but it would've made too many headlines because suddenly you got famous. Now they want you dead even more because of the Social Media thing, but they can't do it without a really good story and someone to blame." He touches his smooth chin and looks at me. "Still don't understand how you got famous without really doing anything," he mutters.

"Nobody understands it," I say with a grin. "Hey, do you mind if I get a picture of . . . never mind. It can wait."

The man turns off the killer look and glances at Xyla. "You're in danger too," he says. "But only if they get to Xavier."

"What?" says Xyla. "Why?"

The man strokes his cheek. "Because you're the patsy," he says like it's no big thing. "Like Lee Harvey Oswald or the guy who killed the other Kennedy. They have to plant someone to take the fall."

My eyes almost fall out of my head as I listen to my dead uncle's bodyguard-boyfriend talk about America's most beloved conspiracy theories. "So as long as I don't get killed, she's safe because they need her in case I *do* get killed?"

"Exactly," says the man, his gray eyes shining. He turns to Xyla, who's starting to look scared if not completely sober yet. "You're the perfect patsy, as bad as that sounds. Orphan. Unmarried. Childless. Career down the tubes. No boyfriend in three years. Friends avoid your calls."

Xyla's mouth hangs open and she balls her fingers into tight fists. I'm tempted to see if she swings at him but decide I'd better intervene. "All right. Enough of that," I snap. Xyla glances at me and I see the color in her cheeks. It's no longer from the wine. She's embarrassed, and although I'm pissed off at the insensitivity of this guy, I'm also kinda kicked that she cares enough about what I think to be embarrassed. Does that make sense? Fuck, does *any* of this make sense?

"What's the motive? How would they frame her?" I say. "Why would she kill me? There's no motive. You might as well just have me shot by a sniper and dumped in the Thames and let the conspiracy theories rage on. I kinda like that, actually. Living forever as a conspiracy theory. Take my place in American history alongside Elvis, Prince, and JFK."

Xyla and the man roll their eyes at me together. Then they look at each other and the man looks down. He isn't looking at the floor, though. He's looking at my wrist.

I groan and slap my wrist where my Rolex should be. "The blonde from the hotel room bar," I mutter. "She was MI-6 too. Fuck. Blondie would go public about spending a night with me. Then Clip-on

Lawyer would kill me. MI-6 would plant the story that Xyla and I fell in love and she lost her shit and murdered me in a jealous rage." I rub my beard and glance at Xyla. "You bad, *bad* girl," I whisper with a wink and a smirk. Then I jump back in glee when she swipes at me. "How would you do it, Xyla? Choke me with my choker? Poke me with the poker? Drown me in wine? Burn me in the bedroom?"

She exhales like a tea-kettle and crosses her arms under her boobs and tightens her jaw. "I've never been more insulted in my life," she says. "And by my own government! How is this OK?"

The man shrugs and checks his nails. They're short and clean like a serial killer. "It's very much *not* OK, Miss Xyla," he says. "That's why I'm here." He glances around the old kitchen like he knows it well. He sighs and his eyes soften for a moment. "Or rather, it's why I'm *still* here. Even though Edward's gone." He looks at me and his gray eyes shine moist and warm. He doesn't say anything.

"I'm glad you're here," Xyla says softly. She touches his arm and looks at me. There's a hint of a smile on her lips, a touch of hurt in her eyes. She straightens up and stiffens her mouth. "So what do we do?" she asks the man. "We can't take on the British Secret Service. If they want to kill Xavier to protect England's reputation and frame me for it, how do we stop them?"

The man takes a breath and exhales slowly. He looks at her and then at me. "There's only one way to stop them. You need to make them *want* to stop."

I think a moment. "You mean make them not want to kill me at all. How do I do that?"

"You know how," says the man quietly.

My phone buzzes just then and I feel it vibrate against my thigh. I close my eyes and shake my head. "I need to be a good Duke," I say through gritted teeth. "Toe the line like a good doggie. Don't poop on the carpet. Don't swing from the curtains. Don't whip the masses into a feeding frenzy. Fuck that. It's what I do. I stop that and I might as well be dead."

"If you don't stop that you *will* be dead," he says with a shrug, Then he glances at Xyla. When he turns back to me there's that softness in his eyes again. "And so will she."

I frown and shake my head. "You said they'd just try to frame her."

"They will. But they won't let her live to see a trial. Who knows what could come out if a real lawyer gets interested in the case. Sorry, kids. They'd plant the story, and then, after the news fades . . ." He runs his finger along his throat and shrugs.

The old kitchen goes quiet and it's just the gurgle of the pipes in the walls and the ticking of the grandfather clock in the hall. Xyla touches her throat and takes a step toward the kitchen window. It's dark as pitch outside. Clearly Uncle Ed didn't believe in lawn lights. Is there even a lawn outside? Looked like woods when I checked.

"But you're here talking to us . . ." Xyla says. "Won't anyone watching know that you've betrayed MI-6?"

He shakes his head. "I am the official Secret Service bodyguard to the Duke of Dorshire. Edward's gone but my assignment still stands." He glances at me and then back at Xyla. "So it's perfectly reasonable for me to be here talking to you both. Nobody would suspect anything." He shrugs. "Unless they've been listening."

"How do you know they're *not* listening?" I say, surprised at his nonchalance.

He snorts like he's insulted. "I've swept this manor for electronic surveillance and electro-magnetic frequencies harder than a scullerymaid does the floor."

"Is a scullerymaid the same as a minutemaid?" I ask. Xyla giggles but the man seems puzzled. Perhaps he thinks it was a real question. I gotta figure out this British humor bullcrap.

My choker tickles my throat and I reach for the clasp again. This time I get my fingers down near the latch but it feels stuck. I push and pull, and suddenly something pops off in my hand. It's small and round and cold like metal. It's not a diamond, and when I hold it up to the light it blinks red.

"What the fuck?" I say, frowning at the tiny piece of metal that was lodged in my choker. Suddenly my mind sweeps back to last night. "Blondie!" I gasp. "She must have planted a listening-bug on my—"

But I'm interrupted by a crisp clink that sounds like a hole being punched in glass. I whip my head towards the window and frown when I see a neat round circle in the dark glass. Then I hear a soft crash, and when I see the man in the French suit crumple to the stone floor, a fresh red spot perfectly placed above the brass buttons of his waistcoat, I grab Xyla and pull her to the floor, shielding her with my body as I wait for another pop that will end this scene.

Now I'm scared, I think as I drape my cape over us and we huddle together. But I'm not scared for myself, I realize as I feel Xyla shiver against me like a kitten. I'm scared for her.

Scared of what I feel for her.

Scared of what I'm ready to do for her.

7
XYLA

They aren't going to do anything to us," Xavier whispers in the warm darkness beneath his cape. His breath smells sweet like wine and his body is heavy with a musk that mixes well with the danger in the air.

We huddle together and stay quiet. The water-pipes make a comforting gurgle in the walls, and the clock in the hall clicks with a relaxing solemness. I should be scared but I'm not. Yes, I'm sad for the old bodyguard who was also Duke Edward's lover and partner, but it's a melancholy sort of sadness, the kind of sadness where you know someone's ending fits his story.

"Remember what he told us," Xavier murmurs, his voice deep and delicate. There's a protective energy coming from him that's surprising and powerful. It's cozy under this cape, and even though it's laughable that fake-fur could stop a bullet, I feel oddly secure. I've never felt secure in my life, it occurs to me suddenly. I tell myself I'm drunk and just saw a man die and there's no way I can be thinking clearly. So why do I feel clear like a sunny sky in the morning, like a new day is dawning, a new life is forming? Also, why am I smiling?!

I nod, thankful that it's dark and he can't see my smile. "Right. They can't just pop you in the head with a military sniper rifle if they want to frame me for your murder. They'd have to use an ice-pick or some household item. Should we get up then? Perhaps hide all the ice-picks and sharp objects to confound the assassins?"

Xavier chuckles and I giggle. He makes no move to get up off me. He's weighing me down like one of those heavy blankets that make you feel like you're back in the womb and safe from the monsters. I think of that painting and wish I'd asked the man about it. Then I think of Blondie and want to ask Xavier about it.

A flush of heat rises up my neck and fills my

cheeks, and at first I wonder if it's honest-to-goodness jealousy. But it's not jealousy. It's worse. In fact it's so much worse that I wish it *were* jealousy. After all, jealousy is a mix of insecurity and anger, and I can get past those emotions. But this is different. It's different because it's more complicated than jealousy, more destructive than anger, more insidious than insecurity.

Disappointment always is.

"Listen, Xyla," he says. "I didn't fuck her."

"Good to know," I say, my reply coming far too quickly. Does he know I was thinking about that? Why is *he* thinking about it? "But you don't need to explain."

"I *want* to explain," he says, shifting his weight off me and slowly pulling the cape back. The kitchen light is dim but it still makes me squint.

Xavier's sitting back on his knees, stroking his chin and frowning. I glance toward the dark window, holding my breath and wondering if MI-6 will just say to hell with framing anyone and let's just kill them both and bury them in the woods. Then I hear Xavier's phone vibrate and I remember why MI-6 can't just "disappear" a Social Media Star without a story.

"You know what's funny?" I say, struggling up and

somehow managing to get my big thighs crossed to where it's vaguely comfortable. "Your fame is the reason why they want to kill you and it's also the reason why they *can't* kill you. Not without a good cover story, anyway."

"Hey, is that British irony?" Xavier says, pulling out his phone and grinning as he unlocks it with his thumb. He glances at the dead body and then at the window. The bullethole is nice and neat, with those little cracks that make it look picture-perfect. Xavier poses near the bullethole and snaps a selfie. I shake my head and wonder what the world has come to when people will *LIKE* and *LOVE* and *OMG* and *WTF* the picture without really stopping to consider whether it's real or not. It's all real in that virtual world, isn't it. We might as well be living in that painting.

"Should we call someone? I feel we should call someone." I look at the man's body. His face is calm and smooth in death. The blood is cherry-red and I consider tasting it to make sure it isn't fake. Now I wonder if it *is* fake, and I hold my breath and watch the man's chest. It doesn't move. He's dead. This is real.

Xavier glances at the body. "Nah," he says. "Let's just leave it here. They'll clean it up once we're out of the way." He chuckles when he sees my expression. "I mean when we leave the kitchen. Come on."

"Where are we going?" I say, clambering to my knees and wincing because my left foot isn't cooperating. "Thanks," I say when Xavier helps me up.

We both glance at the window and then look around the room. No laser-sight dots. I notice how Xavier's standing between me and the window. Would he really take a bullet for me? I look up at him and swallow. He smiles and takes my hand in his. It makes me feel warm and nice but I pull my hand away.

"It's dark and we have no transport," I say, forcing myself to focus.

"We don't need transport. We aren't going anywhere."

I glance at the body. The blood is still very red. "You said we'd leave so they can clean up the body."

"I said we'd leave the kitchen. And we will. Come on. Let's go upstairs."

"All right."

We leave the kitchen and walk slowly up the grand oak staircase. The banister is smooth and polished. The first floor hallway is wood-paneled and dark. Portraits of past Dukes and Duchesses line the walls. I imagine our own painted faces on the walls and glance over at Xavier and then down at the red runner carpet.

Now there are sounds from the kitchen, and I grab Xavier's arm. The back door creaks. We stop and listen. A soft grunt and low voices. Then the back door closes and all is quiet. Xavier and I look at each other as the solemn portraits look at us.

"Something isn't right," I say.

"You're very perceptive."

I smack his arm and smile. "I mean why aren't they storming up the stairs to finish this like the man said? We're both here now. My fingerprints are all over the house." I run my tongue over my lips and glance down at my bosom. I don't say it but I think it and feel it. Our DNA is all over each other after that kiss. We're walking petri-dishes. Easy picking for a forensics lab. They could write any story they want. It's all here for the telling. Why aren't they strolling up the stairs to finish us off?

Xavier's phone vibrates and he looks at it and grins. I stare at his expression and then reach for my satchel before remembering that it's down in the wine cellar. Xavier's posting something else, and his phone is going nuts. I glance down the stairs as curiosity creeps up my spine. Before I can stop myself I'm running down the stairs like someone's after me.

I stumble down into the dark cellar and find my satchel. My phone comes out and I furiously check Xavier's postings. My eyebrows arch as I read, and by the time I get back to where Xavier's still posting, my eyes burn from not blinking enough.

I read the caption beneath the bullethole pic: *You missed, Your Highness!*

Then one of the hallway of portraits with Xavier cross-eyed and his tongue hanging out: *Do I still get a spot on the wall if I'm assassinated by the Queen?*

"Are you mad?" I say. "What are you doing?"

"Staying alive," he says without looking up from his phone. "Check this one out. Did I spell it right?"

Won't bend the knee but will bend the arse! I look up at him and then back at my screen. My head hurts and so does my sense of decency. But yet I can't look away. Clearly millions of others can't either. "Ohmygod. Did you just take that picture when I went down to get my satchel? Is that a picture of your . . . um . . . bottom?"

"Full moon, baby," says Xavier with a wolfish wink. He leans his shaggy head back and howls at the dead Dukes and Duchesses. His excitement is infectious, and I can't help but giggle.

"I don't know whether you're an idiot or a genius," I mutter, scrolling through the comments. New ones are coming in so fast my app can't refresh fast enough. I scan some of the profiles of Xavier's followers. "Huh," I say, checking a few more and then looking up at him like maybe he *is* a genius. "A lot of your new followers are Brits. They're loving this stuff. They're . . . they're loving *you*, Xavier." I look up and then listen for any sounds coming from downstairs. It's all quiet in the manor. Is this actually working? Is it going to *keep* working? Or is it just delaying the inevitable.

"You're only as popular as your last post," Xavier says, his smile thinning like he knows what I'm thinking, like he's thinking it too. "This buys us some time. Maybe not much, but you never know how much time you have. Makes you wonder how to use your time when you don't know how much you have left, right?"

"What are you talking about?" I say.

Xavier shrugs. He turns to me and takes a step towards me. That wolfish grin is back, and I back away from him and shake my head in disbelief. "What are you doing?" I whisper. "No, Xavier. Absolutely not. Are you mad?"

The American Duke saunters towards me, his fake-fur cape looking grand and full. The portraits stretch back to infinity on either side of his broad body, and I feel myself getting drawn into the moment, a moment that feels like it's always been here, waiting for us to get to it, waiting for us to seize it.

Xavier seizes my arm and pulls me into him, wrapping his cape around my shoulders and holding me close. There's something in his green eyes that excites me and scares me, delights me and destroys me. It's that devil-may-care look, that who-gives-a-damn sparkle, that you-only-live-once twinkle. He knows just like I do that shit has gone to bollocks, that we're living in a twisted reality where the real world is as crazy as the invented world. Our lives are at risk because of the fake world of Social Media. But at the same time that's the reason we're still alive. In some screwed-up way, Xavier's thumbs have the power of both life and death over us. It's like one of those myths where the heroes are trapped in some topsy-turvy riddle or chicken-and-egg type catch. You push the boulder up the hill even though you know it's going to roll back down and you'll have to push it up again but you can't stop because if you stop everything stops.

And that's the game of life, isn't it, I think as Xavier touches my hair and caresses my cheek and brings his wine-red lips close to mine. Back and forth and back again and forth again. Like two heroic hamsters running for their damned lives on a wheel suspended above a burning pit. But the little critters are having the time of their lives, their pink tongues hanging out in the joy of the chase, the fury of the flight.

This is why they say it isn't the destination but the journey, I think as Xavier's lips brush against mine and our phones vibrate and our hearts thrum and the assassins' laser-sighted scopes pan the scene and the dead Dukes glare and the dead Duchesses glower.

Because the destination is always the same, comes the thought along with Xavier's kiss.

The story is always the same.

The ending is always the same.

But the way you get there . . . now that's where life is lived.

It's in the details.

In the twists.

In the madness.

In the drama.

In the chaos.

And in the kiss.

The kiss that's here now.

8

XAVIER

The kiss is our third but feels like our first and could be our last. Her lips taste sweet like that old wine, and her curves feel warm against my skin. Our phones buzz like bees in the garden of our love, and I imagine laser-sighted scopes flecking the walls like red starlight in the night-sky of our madness.

We kiss again with a desperation that comes from knowing we're dancing on a tightrope, that my dumbass selfies and lame-ass eyebrow pose got us into this and are the only thing that can get us out. Well, not really get us out. It keeps us alive, but we need to keep dancing on that tightrope to stay alive. The pressure excites me, and I feel Xyla's excitement too. Perhaps it's the moment, the madness, the manor. Maybe it's the danger, the drama, the dread. Come dawn we might be nervous wrecks calling everyone from the CIA to the KGB while praying to every god with a name, every goddess with a face. But tonight we're in this upside-down world where my fake-fur is mink and my diamonds are rhinestones and this kiss is the only thing right, the only thing real, the only thing that exists.

And so I give myself to the kiss and I give myself to her. The walls close in on us and then fade into blackness, and she's so warm and wet against my mouth I want to swallow her whole like maybe I am a monster. We both smile through the kiss and pull back for air and bump noses as we go back into each other. My hands slide down her back and rest on her bottom. She tightens and I stiffen, and now I'm kissing her neck and kneading her ass and grinding against her front. I pull her to the floor, whipping off my cape and spreading it on the red runner carpet that's now the royal bedroom.

"Just so you know it's an option, I think all those doors lead to bedrooms," Xyla says, blushing as I prop myself on my arms above her and let my gaze travel down her neck and rest on her bosom.

"I want you here. In front of these dead Dukes and Duchesses," I whisper.

She looks past me and frowns at a particularly stern, obscenely jowly Duke from the 1600s. Then she shrugs and loops her arms around my neck. "If the Queen hears of it she may decide that it's off with our heads."

"Can she do that?" I say, kissing Xyla's neck as I inquire about the Queen's ability to bestow death sentences.

"No," Xyla says, arching her neck back. I run my tongue along her neckline and she gasps. "If she could I think she'd have done it to about three of our Prime Ministers by now."

"Oh, you bad little Brit," I growl. "I'd like to Prime you and Minister myself inside." She giggles as I growl again, undoing her top button and then the next and finally losing my patience and snapping the rest of her buttons as I pull open her blouse. Her cleavage is big and bodacious and my face is in there and I'm ravaging the soft space between her globes even as I fumble for the bra-clasp. It's beneath her and I don't want to get my face out from her warm bosom and so I firmly grasp the underwire and pull it apart at the middle. Then I rip the satin to shreds and yank it off her. I sniff her scent from each warm bra-cup and then toss the bra. It lands beneath a scowling portrait of a Duchess. I smile and turn my attention back to my own Duchess.

The sight of her nipples big like dinner plates and red like plums makes me gloss over the thought, but when I take her left breast into my mouth and suck it gently and then harder, it occurs to me that an American Duke taking a British Duchess would be a whole new stream of Social Media madness. After all, everyone loves a royal wedding. Shouldn't matter if it's the Duke of Dumblefuck marrying a commoner. Hell, in this day and age of anti-one-per-centers, we'd be the toast of Twitter!

"We're going to be married," I gurgle into her boobs as I move from one breast to the other. She gasps and arches her neck and shudders as I suck. Then she grabs a fistful of my hair and pulls my head back.

"Excuse me?"

"You heard me," I pant, moving down along her smooth round curves and circling her belly button with my filthy tongue. "Shit, you have a dynamite shape, Xyla. You're gonna look great all knocked up in a wedding gown."

I undo the button on her black slacks and she reaches down and grabs my hands. I rest my bearded chin on her mound and look up at her and grin. Her scent rises to me through her pants and underwear, and I lose the smile and get dangerously close to losing control.

"Don't say things you don't mean," she says as I press my face into her crotch and breathe deep and long. Her musk is thick and feminine, clean and warm, and I slowly unzip her and then groan as her scent floods my nostrils. I'm so hard I'm oozing into my boxers, and if I don't fuck her now I might explode in my pants.

"I never say things I don't mean," I mutter as I roll her slacks down her hips and stare like a horny schoolboy at her beige panties that are wet at the crotch. I can see her bush through the soaked satin, and it takes my arousal to the fucking stratosphere. "Fuck, you are so sexy. I'm so glad you don't wax your pussy. I bet the Queen doesn't either. Royal bush all the way. Smells so good. I need a taste of my Duchess."

I feel the blush go through her body like a wave, and when I pull her panties down her slit is gleaming with wetness. Fuck, she's so turned on I almost pass out, and my eyelids flutter like a fool as I lean in and lick her carefully, the flat of my tongue tasting her with long upward strokes.

She's oozing wetness and I'm lapping it up with glee, and when I pull back her dark hood and press my tongue tight on her clit, she bucks her hips and grabs my hair and comes in my face like she can't help herself.

"Oh, goodness!" she gasps, almost scalping me as she yanks my hair and hunches forward and then slams back down onto my soft cape. I open my mouth wide like a walrus and devour her clit and pussy while sliding my palms under her and spreading her bottom and pressing my middle finger against her clean rear rim. She tightens and gasps and then comes hard again into my face, her pussy squirting all over my lips and beard and nose. I gasp and grin and lick my lips and slide that middle finger up her asshole, making her convulse and curse and come again like a good little English girl.

She thrashes and groans and then goes still. I look up from her bush and see her gorgeous breasts moving up and down like the Falkland Islands. I almost make the comment out loud. She'd probably get the Falkland Islands reference. Not sure if she wants to think about Margaret Thatcher right now, though. Why am I thinking about Margaret Thatcher? Do I have a secret fetish for Prime Ministers?

"Oh, goodness," she whispers, blinking and looking up at the ceiling. She gulps a breath and bites her lip. Then she looks down and sees my wet face and turns bright plum. "Did I do that? Ohmygod, I'm so, *so* sorry! I'm mortified! I didn't know women could do that!"

I lick my lips and grin. "It's considered a sign of true love amongst the American people," I say with a wink. Now I move up along her body and kiss her gently on the lips so she can taste herself. She turns her face away but I grip her cheek and face her forward and kiss her deep and long, rolling my tongue inside her mouth until she relaxes and opens up.

"I hardly think we're in the throes of true love, Xavier," she murmurs as I pull back and shift my uncomfortably large erection against her naked mound.

She's looking at those judgmental portraits and I glance at the endless line of solemn semi-royalty with their dead eyes and pale faces. "We're more in love than any of those couples ever were," I say. "Look at them, Xyla. You think those crusty old cretins ever made love on this carpet? Hell, did they even make love?"

Xyla blinks and looks at me. Her lips move like she wants to say something. Her eyes soften and then she looks away like she thought better of it.

I stroke her cheek and narrow my eyes and I know what she's thinking. I know what she wanted to say. I know what she wanted to ask.

"Yes," I say. "We *are* making love. We've been making love since the moment we met. Every look we shared. Every word we said. It's all part of our courtship. All part of our love. All part of our story."

"It's a mad story," she says softly.

"Better mad than bad," I say.

She giggles. "Oh, it's *bad* too."

"*You're* bad."

"Stop being silly. I've never been bad in my entire life."

"You just squirted on my face," I remind her.

She gasps and tries to cover her face but I grab her wrists and shake my head and look her dead on with a seriousness that makes me shudder. "Everything I just said is true. It's true to how I feel, Xyla. I want us to be married. I want you to be my Duchess. And I want you round and pregnant at the wedding."

She studies my face silently and then looks past me at the ceiling. "We met yesterday, Xavier. How can we know so soon? What if it's a mistake?"

I shrug. "Then we have a highly public, grossly messy, majorly over-the-top, stupendously royal divorce." She gasps and grins and I shrug again. "Hell, maybe we'll do that anyway after a couple of years. What? Remember, we'll need to stay in the news or else . . ." I run my finger across my throat and roll my eyes up in my head. I smile but Xyla doesn't laugh.

"Stop that," she says. "I don't want to think about what happens tomorrow or the next day or ever. Oh, Xavier! What are we going to do?"

"We're going to live our lives and do it publicly," I say firmly. "We're bound together now. You can't go back to your old life, Xyla. You know too much now. You step off the stage and they'll make you disappear without bothering about a cover story. I can't let that happen. I won't let it happen. I won't let you go, Xyla. We're in this together now. You and me. We stay in the spotlight and we stay alive. We perform for the audience and the powers that be let us live another day. That's the game, Xyla. And I know how to play it really fucking well. I know how to stand up and say *Look at me* like nobody else can. And you're going to learn it too. I'll teach you, Xyla. It's like learning how to dance. Just follow my lead and you'll do fine. They'll love you, Xyla. I sure as hell do."

The words pour from a place that I know is different from where I draw my superficial bullshit, and I see that I'm getting to her. But not just that: I'm getting to me too. I believe every word I just said.

Especially those last few words.

"I love you, Xyla," I whisper. "You have to believe that. It's the only way we're going to get through this. From now on our whole lives are going to be scripted and rehearsed, played out in front of the Social Media audience who are fickle and cruel, who force you to raise the stakes and will turn their back on you if you aren't outrageous enough or controversial enough or wild enough." I kiss her and smile and kiss her again and draw back. "The only way to live like this is to surrender to it, Xyla. Let the fakeness become real. Let the stage expand to where *everything* is the stage. Then it all becomes real, you see?"

"You're crazy," she whispers, her eyes wide but sparkling with a light that makes me believe . . . makes me believe that she's starting to believe. "But you're also right. I can't just go back to my old life." She takes a breath and blinks and frowns like she's surprised at what she just thought. She blinks again and turns back to me, her eyes firm, her lips tight. "I don't *want* to go back to my old life, Xavier. All right. I'm in. I'll follow your lead. What do I do next?"

She smiles up at me and I laugh down at her. I kiss her nose and her lips, lick her neck and growl between her breasts. Then I prop myself up on my arms and move my hips against hers. She looks down between us and her eyes go wide and her lips tremble. I kiss her once more and then guide her hand towards the royal bulge, the sovereign scepter, the Duke's dongle.

9
<u>XYLA</u>

You aren't the Duke yet," I remind him as my fingers close around his thick shaft over his trousers. He feels so big in my hands that I'm excited again even though I just came with mortifying messiness.

Xavier grunts and guides my other hand to his crotch. Then he goes up on his knees and straddles me, spreading his arms out wide like Richard the Lionheart speaking to the people. His cape is now our bed, but he's still got that ridiculous choker on his neck and those American biker boots on his feet. Not to mention that scepter in his pants.

"Careful with the zipper," he whispers as I undo his belt and pop the top button of his dark wool trousers. "One scratch on the sword and you'll spend your days in my dungeon."

"Is that a threat or a bribe?" I tease, pulling down the zipper with a quickness that makes Xavier's eyes pop. I giggle when he exhales. Then I gasp when he growls and shakes his long index finger at me with fake disapproval that feels so real I suddenly understand what he means by surrendering to the fakeness, making our whole lives a stage—even the private parts of our lives.

Maybe *especially* the private parts.

"You just risked Dorshire's most valuable asset," Xavier says with that trademark eyebrow-raise and a fake British accent that's deep and debonair and makes me laugh and makes me wet. He glances up at the silent Dukes. "Wouldn't you agree, chaps?" He cocks his head and nods and then looks down at me. "They agree," he says solemnly. Now he looks up at the Dukes again and raises both eyebrows. "Really? Oh, you filthy old bastards. Is that how you disciplined the chambermaids and scullerymaids and minutemaids? What, what is a minutemaid? Really? How droll." I'm already snickering now, and when Xavier looks down his nose at me like he really is a stodgy old Duke with a filthy private mind, I can't hold back the laugh as he says, "Speaking of droll, it's time for you to roll. Come on. Turn over. Raise your ass. Oh, excuse me. Your *arse*."

He moves back on his knees, and the motion makes his cock push through the slit in his boxers. He's enormous, and he's so damned hard that the spring-release sprays a thick line of pre-cum along my naked body, marking me from mound to mouth with his clear warm oil. I gasp and stare at the massive head that's dark red and shiny. The shaft is thick like a tree and twice as long, and my gaze follows it back to where I see the outline of balls heavy and large pushing against his underwear. I gulp and glance up at him. His lips are fixed in a wolfish grin, and he's looking at my mouth like he's imagining something filthy and delicious.

I'm imagining it too, and our eyes meet and now he pulls back and plonks himself down on his butt and feverishly pulls off his boots and yanks off his trousers and rips off his underwear. Then he's straddling me again and I'm gasping again when he drags his cockhead up along my belly and circles my nipples, leaving them sticky red and pointy hard before he gets to my chin.

I look down along his length and then up into his eyes. He's lean but broad, and he towers above me in a way that exudes power. The light comes from behind and casts his face in shadow. I see green eyes and golden light flickering through his mussed hair and ruffled beard. Behind him those old Dukes gaze upon us, and as I stroke my Duke's cock and massage his balls I feel myself surrendering more and more, yielding to this strange pull that beckons me to a world of vivid fakeness, a realm of raw romance, a wonderland of filthy fantasy.

Xavier groans as I part my lips for him, and I close my eyes and take him inside. He's so thick my mouth stretches at the seams, and I gag and gurgle as he pushes down my throat with firm authority and holds himself there. I breathe noisily through my nose, and I'm so wet between my legs it feels warm and sticky. Those heavy balls are against my chin, and his masculine musk is as deep inside me as his cock.

"You all right?" he whispers, tracing his fingertips along my cheek and past my ear. I nod and he smiles and I tighten as he slides his fingers through my hair and takes firm hold.

Then he starts to move, and my eyes bulge as arousal thick and filthy floods me with a need that's frighteningly fantastical. Suddenly I want to be owned and claimed, held down and fucked like the scullerymaid who sticks her skirted rump in the air when the Duke walks into the kitchen to get an apple. *Look at my rosy-red apples*, she whispers in her mind as the Duke scowls at her rump and then unbuckles his riding breeches.

Xavier drives his shaft down my throat and I see that he's lost in a filthy fantasy of his own. I decide it's the same fantasy, and I suck him hard and pull on his balls and tickle his thighs as he groans and grunts and goes harder and deeper. Now I think of the chambermaid stooping to sweep under the bed, the musk of her unwashed cunt heavy in the air when the Duke strolls in to get something. He gets something all right.

I giggle at my dirty mind, and I swallow a dollop of the Duke's pre-cum mixed with my saliva. Now the fantasy makes me the Duchess, frustrated and lonely, undersexed and annoyed. Does she wander to the stables to watch the help handle the horses? Does she imagine big rough hands down her drawers, thick dirty fingers plunging into her pussy, hard heavy cocks driving into her bottom as the stable-men take turns pleasing the Mistress of the Manor, filling her until she overflows all day and doesn't walk right for weeks?

I feel the secrets on the portaited walls. I hear the murmurs of the silent and the dead. Then suddenly I gasp as my pussy tightens and releases, and I blow hard through my nose and arch my neck back when I realize I just came again without being touched! I choke and gag and I'm about to pull out but Xavier holds my hair so tight it hurts and rams down into me and bellows like a beast and then *explodes* down my throat!

I scream as hot semen floods me, and I pull away and scream again. Semen and saliva spurts from my mouth, and somehow I'm still coming, coming hard and deadly. Xavier's still coming too, and now he staggers back and flips me over and spanks me hard and good on each cheek.

I howl as the smacks ring out like whipcracks. I wail as the Duke spanks me again and spits on my filthy asshole and fingers me deep and long, curling his finger up the Duchess's anus as he slaps her rump again. Then with his finger still in my rear, he drives his spurting cock up my cunt and finishes in me. Deep in me. All the way deep. So deep it feels unreal.

Beautifully unreal.

Fabulously fake.

Miraculously make-believe.

"Bloody hell," he groans as he slaps my ass once more and groans out the last of his seed. I'm snorting like a mare being run to death, and I feel like I'm overflowing from every damned hole. It's so filthy I feel like I just became someone else.

And when Xavier collapses on me and buries his bearded face in my untamed hair, I exhale with a shudder, my breath signaling my surrender, my acquiescence, my release. Somehow I know I just took my place amongst these portraits. Except I'm still alive. I *am* alive, aren't I?

Now there's a noise in the house and Xavier tenses up and suddenly he gets up off me and I'm startled. I turn and pull his cape over my naked body. We both listen. The sound comes again. Footsteps, slow and steady. Now a metallic click. Footsteps again. Closer now. Coming up the stairs. Slowing down to a crawl. Another clink of metal.

"Get to that bedroom and lock the door," he commands, smiling and cupping my cheek when he sees my panic. Only now does Xavier realize I'm not looking at him. I'm looking past him, towards the ominous sound of metal clicking in the night.

"Damned clip-on ties never stay on right," comes the voice, and Xavier whips around and jumps to his feet. He spreads his arms out wide and stands above me as I cower under his cape. Xavier's naked and I peer between his legs and see a bald-headed man fiddling with his clip-on tie.

Clip-on Lawyer curses again and struggles and finally he pulls off the fake tie. The metal tie-clip clicks one last time as he tosses it away with satisfaction that seems like it was building up in him for a while.

"I'm warning you, I won't go down easy," Xavier growls. He clenches his fists and I think even his big balls tighten. His cock hangs long between his legs. He's still dripping. It's so ridiculous that it only makes me believe in Xavier more completely. It only makes me surrender to his over-the-top fakeness more willingly.

It only makes me love him more violently.

I pull the cape over my shoulders and around my breasts. Then I lean forward and poke my head out between my Duke's long legs. He looks down at me and frowns, and I wriggle my big body through and stand up. I place my hands on my hips and stare down Clip-on Lawyer as he reaches into his jacket, undoubtedly going for his shoulder-weapon.

"You'll have to shoot me to get to him," I say firmly. "And you can't shoot me if you're trying to frame me."

Clip-on Lawyer frowns and then chuckles and shakes his head. He slowly takes his hand out from his jacket. He's holding something but I can't see what. He leans slightly to his left and closes one eye like he's checking a line of sight.

"I could put one in the side of your head and make it look self-inflicted," he says matter-of-factly. "Then two in the Duke's chest. A couple of stray shots in the wall." Now he glances at Xavier's package and shrugs. "And one in the royal jewels just for dramatic effect." He winks at Xavier. "Don't worry, mate. I'd kill you first. I'm not a sadist." He frowns and glances past us like maybe he's rethinking the sadist comment. Then he chuckles and tosses whatever he was holding at us.

Xavier steps in front of me and catches it. He looks at it and groans. It's his Rolex watch.

"Seriously?" he says to Clip-on Lawyer. "You pick right now to toss me something that can only cause unnecessary drama? Who wrote this fucking script? This is worse than *Stripper-Housewives of Atlantic City*." He turns to me naked and guilty. "Look, babe. Blondie didn't mean a thing. We never even fucked. Hell, I was so drunk I doubt I'd have even been *able* to fuck her."

"Is that supposed to make me feel better?" I demand, stifling a smile as a perverse sense of indignant fun ripples through me. Now I understand why people love watching reality-show drama even when they know it's staged. It's the same reason Englishfolk love the queen and love the pomp and love the splendor even though it's laughable and outdated. There's something about surrendering to the fiction, becoming part of the script, joining in the game, pretending like it's real.

Pretending so hard it *becomes* real, I think as we face off for a fake fight that feels like fun, so much fun it *has* to be real.

And you know what, I think as I lay into him and he grovels and apologizes and we go back and forth with the glee of those hamsters running in earnest. Yes, you know what? It is real.

Real and I love it.

Love the drama.

Love the madness.

Love the ups.

Love the downs.

Love the always.

And love the forever.

10

SIX WEEKS LATER
BUCKINGHAM PALACE
XAVIER

"I waited forever for this moment," Xyla whispers as we bow our heads and wait for the Queen's royal procession to exit the Grand Hall. "And it was grander than I could have imagined. She is *such* a darling, isn't she? *So* graceful. I can't believe she invited us here as a couple even though we aren't married and the news just broke that I'm . . . well . . ."

She glances at her belly that isn't showing yet but soon will. Then we glance at each other and I raise my left eyebrow as my beard twitches with a stifled smile. "The threat of a bastard child looms large over the British Empire," I whisper ominously as Xyla turns purple trying not to laugh. "Whatever will they do? Will they legitimize the child or allow it to be born out of wedlock. Born a *bastard*."

"You like saying the word *bastard* in a British accent, don't you?" she says as the Queen's footmen (or minutemen—who the hell knows) direct us towards the archway leading to the Great Lawn in the back where they'll serve Earl Gray tea and cucumber-butter sandwiches—the latter of which I think is probably the unspoken reason for the American revolution. Isn't bad cucumber sandwiches the reason for the Boston Tea Party?

"I'm considering delaying the wedding until you give birth just so we can have a legitimate bastard child," I say.

"A legitimate bastard?" she says as we stroll out into the wide hallways where white-gloved men in regalia stand in polite circles and women in jewels and gowns pretend to sip from empty teacups. "Isn't that an oxymoron?"

"*What* did you call me?" I growl, grabbing her gloved arm and stopping near a side hallway that leads to we know not where. "I'm a real Duke now, remember. And you're still the scullerymaid."

She chuckles. "I thought I was the minutemaid."

I pull her inappropriately close and look at her with very appropriate warmth. "You're the Duchess, Xyla. My Duchess. My woman. My forever." Then I raise my left eyebrow and tilt my head towards the hallowed hallways of Buckingham. "This'll just take a minute, though. Come on."

She blinks three times and looks at me like I'm mad. "We can't," she whispers. She tries to pull away but I've got her by the arm and we duck into the hallway. It's a dark hallway, and we both gasp when we see that it's lined with portraits of England's former Kings and Queens dating back to when the years were only three digits.

"Oh, but we *must*," I whisper. I kiss her hard on the lips and squeeze her big bottom as she gasps and pushes and pulls and then surrenders.

And now she kisses me back and I cup her newly pregnant belly and slide my hand between her legs. She's already wet for me, and I'm so fucking hard I'm dizzy like a Duke should be. It occurs to me that there are almost certainly cameras covering every square inch of Buckingham Palace. She knows it too, I realize when I see the glint in my minutemaid's eyes.

A glint that first emerged when we surrendered

to each other and to our story in that old manor.

A glint that's only gotten brighter over the past few weeks, as Xyla learned how to play the game, how to make love to the camera, speak with her eyes, tease with her smile. She's learning how to say *Look at me* without speaking a word. She's learning how Social Media stars are like royalty, all pomp and pretense, splendor without substance, fakeness with flourish.

But this . . . I think when I raise her gown and take her deep and kiss her hard and feel her love.

This isn't fake.

It can't be faked.

It won't be faked.

Because it's the only thing that's real in this story.

The only thing that was ever real in this story.

The only reason there's a story at all.

∞

EPILOGUE
FIVE YEARS LATER
XYLA

"**H**ow's this?" Xavier says, flashing his perfect smile while doing that eyebrow raise.

I close an eye and shake my head. "Nah. Doesn't feel right. Try another."

The portrait artist sighs and looks at his blank easel. He's too polite to say it, but his expression says, "Pick a pose! For love of Queen and Country, pick a damned pose!"

I glance over at the other portrait artist. She's so annoyed she's glaring at her nails. I know she's imagining crushing my skull between her fingers.

The two of them have watched the two of us argue over portrait-poses for most of the day now. We've been taking pictures and posting them online for feedback from our fans. Naturally nobody can agree. They never agree. If they agree, it gets lame and everyone leaves and the party's over. I don't think MI-6 still has that plan dangling out there, but you never know. Clip-on Lawyer is now our official bodyguard, but maybe he turns assassin the moment the Social Media lights go out. So we gotta keep the plates spinning, keep the balls in the air, keep making the commoners look at us twenty times a day for a dopamine hit.

But the truth is, the drama has become a drug to us too. We're so deep into the game that it's just second nature to raise the stakes, to see how far we dare to take it. We're so bold now it's scary, and it's hard to imagine we're still here five years later. After all, when secret security footage from Buckingham Palace got leaked five years ago I thought we were done for, that we'd grow old in the Queen's dungeons. But no. It spread so fast and people loved the playful defilement so much the Queen pretended like it never happened.

Though of course Xavier insists she watches it with the entire Royal family on Saturday nights.

Eating Spotted Dick and Head Sausage, he likes to say drolly. Overdone jokes but they still make me smile.

"You know what?" I suddenly say as Xavier rubs his jaw which must hurt from so many fake smiles. "No smiles. That's why our poses feel wrong. I mean, look at the rest of these Dukes and Duchesses. They're jowly and scowly, long-nosed and turtle-necked. Come on. Let's see some jowls. Let's have us a scowl. Show off that neck-skin."

Xavier chuckles but then stops when he sees I'm serious. He glances up at the rows of solemn portraits, and when he looks back at me I know he just got taken back to that first night, when we surrendered to our story.

"You see it, don't you?" I whisper as we stroll hand in hand down the hallway as the portrait-artists prepare the paint. We stop in front of the recent portrait of Duke Edward. I think of his secret life. Then I scan the other faces, and I wonder about their secret lives. Finally I wonder about all the secret lives of the men and women trapped in the roles of royalty, forced to toe the line when perhaps they yearned to be free, to be wild, to live out dreams that were closed to them. Xavier and I can mock and defile and poke fun and play the fool, and people in today's fake-reality world will love on us and cheer on us and throw glitter and gold on us. But what about fifty years from now? A hundred years from now? A thousand? Do we want to be recorded as grinning idiots or do we want to leave one tradition intact, keep up the age-old pretense that there's something sophisticated and solemn about royalty, that we're not like the commoners, never will be . . . even though we are like the commoners, always will be.

And that's the irony, isn't it? It's why commoners love royalty, isn't it? We don't *want* to know they're like us! We don't *want* to know their poop stinks and their pits perspire and they have bad teeth or bald spots or weird knees or bunions on their big toes. We need the veneer to stay shiny, just like we don't want the actor to break from his role because it will break us from our own roles.

And that's what life is about, isn't it, I think as we turn to the portrait artists and show them our poses. Our scowls draw their smiles, and I see their eyes light up in a way that tells me we got it right, that we're playing our roles in this fantasy.

This fantasy that's so real that we don't even call it a fantasy . . .

We just call it life.

∞

FROM THE AUTHOR

I had fun with that! Hope you did too!

More CURVY FOR KEEPS coming up with
SAVING THE SINNER!

And check out my other instalove series: DRAG-
ON'S CURVY MATE andCURVY FOR HIM!

College romance your thing? Try my CURVY IN
COLLEGE Series!

Longer books your thing? Try my 23 full-length
novels: CURVES FOR SHEIKHS and CURVES
FOR SHIFTERS!

And do consider joining my private list at
ANNABELLEWINTERS.COM/JOIN
to get five never-been-published forbidden epi-
logues from my SHEIKHS series.

Love,
Anna.

∞

Printed in Great Britain
by Amazon

20587692R00068